Tessie
Bear

D0709848

HarperCollins *Children's Books*

It was a beautiful, sunny day and Tessie Bear was walking through Toy Town.

"Parp-parp!" said Noddy's little red and yellow taxi as he drew up beside Tessie Bear.

"Hello, Tessie Bear," greeted Noddy. "It's such a lovely day; would you like to join me for a picnic? I've got some tasty sandwiches we can share."

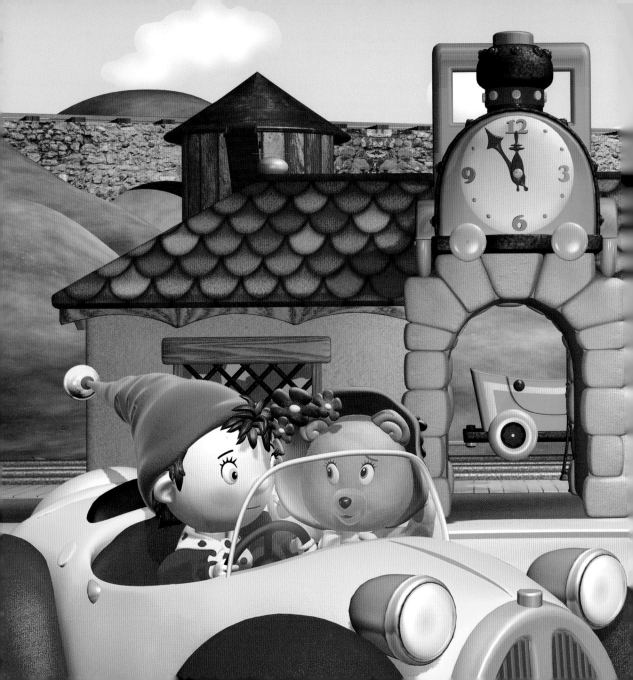

"A picnic is a lovely idea, Noddy!"
said Tessie Bear, happily.
"Let's go to the farm on the way
and collect some fresh milk to drink."

Tessie Bear had just collected some milk from the cow when Noddy looked up and noticed the farm's windmill.

"Look at how fast the windmill is spinning, Tessie!" cried Noddy.

"Oh, let's fly a kite at the picnic! It's perfect weather for kite-flying!" replied Tessie.

By the time the two friends reached
the field and set out the picnic,
the wind had really picked up.

Tessie laid out the picnic blanket,
but the wind kept lifting it into the air!

Noddy tried to light the barbecue,
but the wind kept putting it out!

"It's too windy to eat,"
said Tessie. "The only thing we
can do in this wind is fly the kite!"

Tessie and Noddy started to unravel
the string of the kite. Looking up, Noddy
saw that a rainbow had appeared
in the sky above them.

"What strange weather this is!"
exclaimed Noddy.

Tessie Bear had to hold very tightly
to the string of the kite so that
it did not fly off and escape.

"Look how it's wriggling and jiggling
in the sky! It really wants to play
in the wind," Tessie called to Noddy.

"Hold tight, Tessie!" Noddy warned.
"I don't want to lose my favourite kite!"

Noddy started to pack away
the picnic blanket. He didn't
want it to fly away.

"Oh!" cried Tessie Bear.

"What's that, Tessie?" asked Noddy,
still busily packing his bag.

While Noddy's back was turned, a gust
of wind scooped Tessie Bear up, up and
away! Holding onto the string of the kite,
she was carried higher and higher.

"What *is* it?" Noddy asked
again, turning to look at Tessie Bear.
"Tessie, where have you gone?"
Noddy cried, when he saw that she
and the kite were no longer there.
He was very puzzled.

"I'm up here, Noddy!" called Tessie,
as loudly as she could. But the kite was
carrying her higher and higher and the
wind whisked her words away before
they could reach Noddy.

Tessie Bear looked down at Toy Town.
"Ohhh, it's a very long way back home!"
she said to herself. She held on even more
tightly to the kite string and sang a song.

I'm so very high
Up in the sky!
It's a long way down
To my home in Toy Town.
But the rainbow is near
And its colours so clear –
I like it here, high in the sky!

Meanwhile, Noddy had finally
noticed that Tessie Bear was
disappearing into the
sky with the kite.

"Hold on, Tessie! I'm coming!"
Noddy called, even though Tessie Bear
was too far away to hear him.

He drove to the airport, jumped into
his aeroplane and zoomed into
the sky to try to rescue her.

Tessie Bear's kite was carrying her towards the rainbow. Tessie was excited, as she had never been through a rainbow before.

"This is magical!" she cried. "Toy Town looks even more colourful from up here in the rainbow!"

Looking down, she noticed something golden and twinkly at the bottom of the rainbow.

"It's the pot of gold at the end of the rainbow!"
Tessie Bear cried. "If only I could reach it –
everyone could have free ice creams for days!"

Tessie Bear tried to reach for the pot,
but it was too far away and she
was going higher and higher.

She stretched as far as she could, but inside
the rainbow it looked much closer to her than
it really was. She stretched and stretched
and *stretched* but still couldn't
reach the pot of gold.

Noddy spotted Tessie Bear and the kite,
floating upwards through the rainbow.
He saw her leaning to the side.

"Hold tight, Tessie Bear, I'm coming
to get you!" Noddy called.

Noddy pointed his aeroplane at
the rainbow and sped onwards.

"Noddy!" Tessie Bear cried, as she floated upwards through the rainbow.

Noddy had no time to waste.
He powered his aeroplane forwards, crying, "I'm here, Tessie Bear! Jump in!"

Plop!

Thanks to Noddy's clever flying, Tessie Bear landed neatly in the passenger seat of the plane, safe and sound.

Within minutes, the friends were
back on solid ground again.

"Thank you for rescuing me, Noddy!"
smiled Tessie Bear. "It's a shame I couldn't
reach the pot of gold. Or have our picnic."

"Never mind," said Noddy.
"I've got a purse of gold coins –
let's have an ice cream –
in rainbow colours!"

First published in the UK by HarperCollins Children's Books in 2008

1 3 5 7 9 10 8 6 4 2
ISBN-13: 978-0-00-725900-7
ISBN-10: 0-00-725900-X

Printed and bound in China

Star in your very own PERSONALISED Noddy book!

In just **3** easy steps your child can join Noddy in a Toyland adventure!

1 Go to www.MyNoddyBook.co.uk

2 Personalise your book

3 Checkout!

3 Great Noddy adventures to choose from:

'Your child' Saves Toytown
Soar through a rainbow in Noddy's aeroplane to help him save Toytown.

A Gift for 'your child'
Noddy composes a song for your child in this story for a special occasion.

A Christmas Gift for 'your child'
Noddy composes a song for your child in a Christmas version of the above story.

Visit today to find out more and create your personalised Noddy book!

www.MyNODDYBook.co.uk